190L

W9-APY-788
03/2016

Dear Parents and Educators,

Welcome to Penguin Young Readers! As parents and educators, you know that each child develops at his or her own pace—in terms of speech, critical thinking, and, of course, reading. Penguin Young Readers recognizes this fact. As a result, each Penguin Young Readers book is assigned a traditional easy-to-read level (1–4) as well as a Guided Reading Level (A–P). Both of these systems will help you choose the right book for your child. Please refer to the back of each book for specific leveling information. Penguin Young Readers features esteemed authors and illustrators, stories about favorite characters, fascinating nonfiction, and more!

Tiny Saves the Day

LEVEL **1**

GUIDED READING LEVEL **D**

This book is perfect for an **Emergent Reader** who:
• can read in a left-to-right and top-to-bottom progression;
• can recognize some beginning and ending letter sounds;
• can use picture clues to help tell the story; and
• can understand the basic plot and sequence of simple stories.

Here are some **activities** you can do during and after reading this book:
• Character Traits: One of Tiny's character traits is that he is friendly. Write a list of some of his other traits.
• Sight Words: Sight words are frequently used words that readers must know just by looking at them. They are known instantly, on sight. Knowing these words helps children develop into efficient readers. As you read the story, have the child point out the sight words below.

are	but	good	now	want
be	get	have	this	well

Remember, sharing the love of reading with a child is the best gift you can give!

—Bonnie Bader, EdM
　　Penguin Young Readers program

*Penguin Young Readers are leveled by independent reviewers applying the standards developed by Irene Fountas and Gay Su Pinnell in *Matching Books to Readers: Using Leveled Books in Guided Reading*, Heinemann, 1999.

For all the students at Evergreen
Country Day School —CM

PENGUIN YOUNG READERS
An Imprint of Penguin Random House LLC

Text copyright © 2016 by Cari Meister. Illustrations copyright © 2016 by Richard D. Davis. All rights
reserved. Published by Penguin Young Readers, an imprint of Penguin Random House LLC,
345 Hudson Street, New York, New York 10014. Manufactured in China.

Library of Congress Cataloging-in-Publication Data is available.

ISBN 978-0-448-48293-4 (pbk)   10 9 8 7 6 5 4 3 2 1
ISBN 978-0-448-48294-1 (hc)   10 9 8 7 6 5 4 3 2 1

PENGUIN YOUNG READERS

LEVEL
EMERGENT
READER

1

TiNY Saves the Day

by Cari Meister
illustrated by Rich Davis

Penguin Young Readers
An Imprint of Penguin Random House

This is Tiny.

He is the best dog.

Everyone loves Tiny.

Everyone but Kiki.

Tiny wants to be friends.

He brings Kiki a toy.

Kiki does not want a toy.

He brings Kiki a treat.

Kiki does not want a treat.

He gives Kiki a kiss.

Kiki does not want a kiss.

Tiny is sad.

It's okay, Tiny.

You have a lot of friends.

Oh no!

Kiki is stuck in a tree!

I try to help.

I get a chair.

I get a ladder.

I am still too small.

27

Tiny can help.

Good dog, Tiny!

Now Tiny and Kiki are

friends.

Well, most of the time!